THE CAMPAIGN KID

VINCE CASALE

a Division of Silversmith Press
Houston, TX

Copyright © Vince Casale

All rights reserved.

This book, or parts thereof, may not be reproduced in any form or by any means without written permission from the publisher, except for brief passages for purposes of reviews.

Illustrated by Silversmith Press Creative

The views and opinions expressed herein belong to the author and do not necessarily represent those of the publisher.

ISBN 978-1-961093-64-5 (Softcover Book)

ISBN 978-1-961093-65-2 (Ebook)

To all the "Campaign Kids" in the world.

Once upon a time, there was a boy named Jake.

Jake lived in America. His parents taught him about government and how America chooses its leaders. This is known as politics. Jake loved reading about politics, talking about politics,
and learning about politics.

Jake knew all about voting, campaigns,
and even the Electoral College.

So, when his best friend Ryan decided
to run for class president,
Jake was sure he could help him win.

Jake started by making colorful posters to tell the
kids why they should vote for Ryan.

"How about this?" Jake said, holding up a big sign that read, "Ryan for Class President.
He's got what it takes!"

Jake was proud of his work,
but Ryan wasn't so sure.
"I don't know," Ryan said.
"It sounds a little cheesy."

Jake rolled his eyes. "Of course, it's cheesy. It's politics, Ryan! You've got to catch everyone's attention and be memorable.
Plus, everyone loves CHEESE!"

Ryan laughed, "Okay, you win. Let's go with it."

Next, Jake and Ryan prepared for a debate.
A debate is when the candidates get to share their
views and answer questions in front
of the whole class.

Jake wrote down questions,
and Ryan practiced what he would say.

However, when the big day arrived,
things didn't happen exactly as planned.

Ryan stood in front of the whole class
when Ms. Jones asked,
"Ryan, what is your plan for improving
the school lunch?"

Ryan was so nervous.
He forgot all about school lunch!

Quick as a flash, Jake jumped in.

"Well, Ms. Jones, as Ryan's campaign manager,
I can tell you that we're planning
to introduce a new pizza topping.
It's called 'Ryan's special sauce.'"

The class erupted in laughter.

Even though things didn't go perfectly,
Jake and Ryan didn't give up.

They went around the classroom, passing out flyers and cheering on their friends to vote.

As the big day to vote got closer, it looked like Ryan's competition was getting more votes than he was.

Ryan and Jake were worried that they might lose the election, but they refused to give up.

Ryan had a great idea. He said,
"Let's make a funny video!"

In the video, Jake danced around and encouraged
everyone to vote for Ryan!

Ryan wasn't sure about the idea at first,
but Jake reminded him that even grown-ups
do silly things to get votes, just like kids.
When they do, it lets the voters know
they are just like them!

They shared the video with their friends and soon everyone at school was talking about it.

On the day of the election,
Ryan and Jake were nervous but excited.
They watched as the votes were counted...

…and to their great joy, Ryan won by a landslide!

Jake felt so happy to help his friend win.

He grabbed Ryan's hand and held it in the air while holding up two fingers on the other hand showing the "V" for victory.

The entire school cheered, and from that day on, Jake was known as "The Campaign Kid."

Printed in the USA
CPSIA information can be obtained
at www.ICGtesting.com
LVHW071700180924
791308LV00002B/96